Caillou®

Fresh from the Farm

Text: Kim Thompson
Illustrations: Eric Sévigny, based on the television series

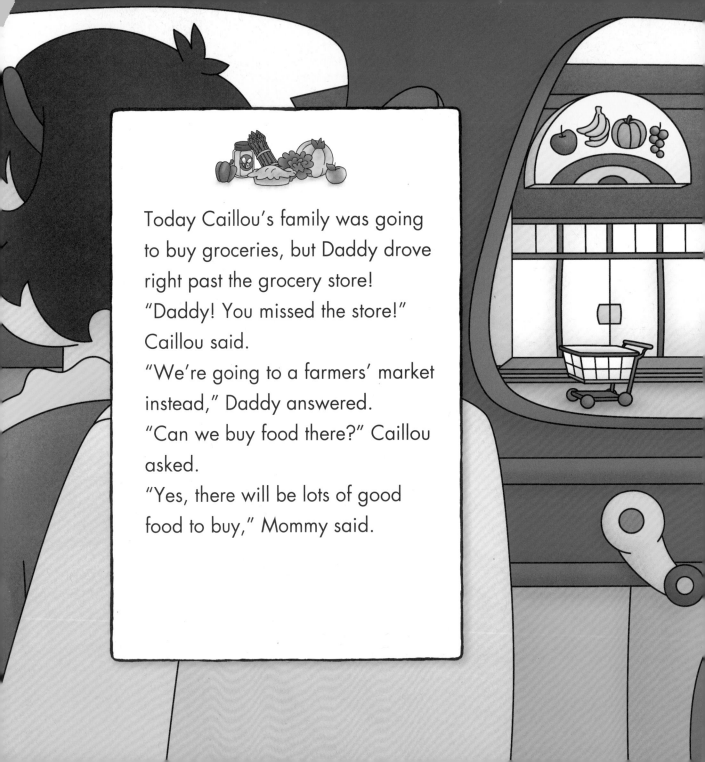

Today Caillou's family was going to buy groceries, but Daddy drove right past the grocery store!

"Daddy! You missed the store!" Caillou said.

"We're going to a farmers' market instead," Daddy answered.

"Can we buy food there?" Caillou asked.

"Yes, there will be lots of good food to buy," Mommy said.

When they arrived, Caillou saw that the farmers' market was very different from the grocery store. The food was all put out on tables.

"Daddy, look. Everything is outside," Caillou said.

"That's right," Daddy said. "The farmers bring the food straight from their farms to the market, so it's really fresh."

Caillou wanted to help, the way he did in the grocery store. He looked for bananas, but couldn't see them anywhere.

"Mommy, where are the bananas?" he asked.

"The farmers' market only has food that is local – that means food that grows nearby," Mommy said.

"Bananas don't grow near here?"
Caillou asked.
"No," Mommy answered.
"Bananas are not local. They
grow so far away that they have
to travel here in a plane."
Caillou thought bananas flying
in a plane must be very funny.

Then Caillou remembered something.

"Strawberries are local! I know because Grandma grows them, and she lives nearby."

"That's right, Caillou," Mommy said.

Caillou looked around. "But I don't see any strawberries."

"They're not ripe until summertime, and it's only spring now," Mommy said.

"We have to wait until summer to buy strawberries, celery, broccoli, peaches, blueberries, raspberries, plums..."

Caillou was getting hungry.

"What can we eat right now?" He wanted to know.

Mommy smiled. "Let's look around at what's available."

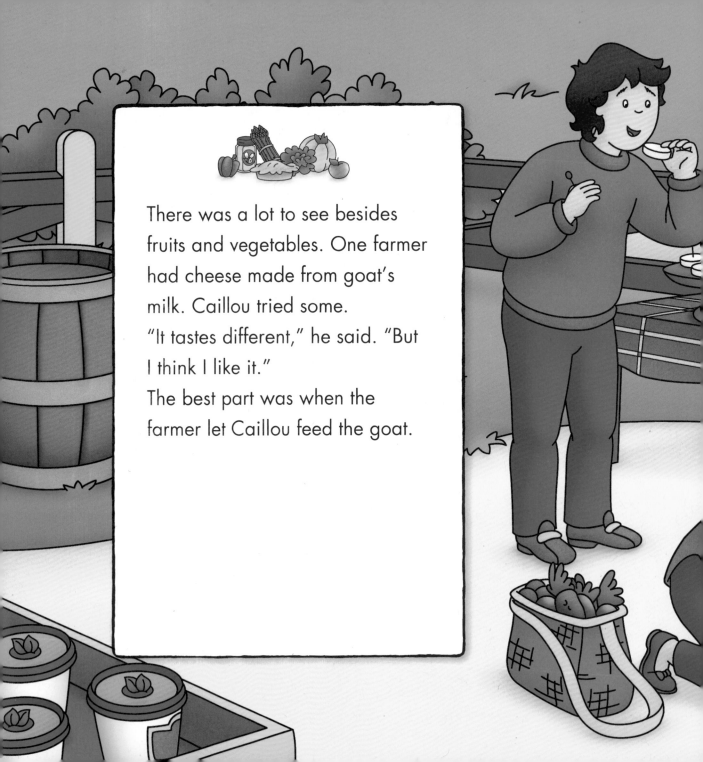

There was a lot to see besides fruits and vegetables. One farmer had cheese made from goat's milk. Caillou tried some.

"It tastes different," he said. "But I think I like it."

The best part was when the farmer let Caillou feed the goat.

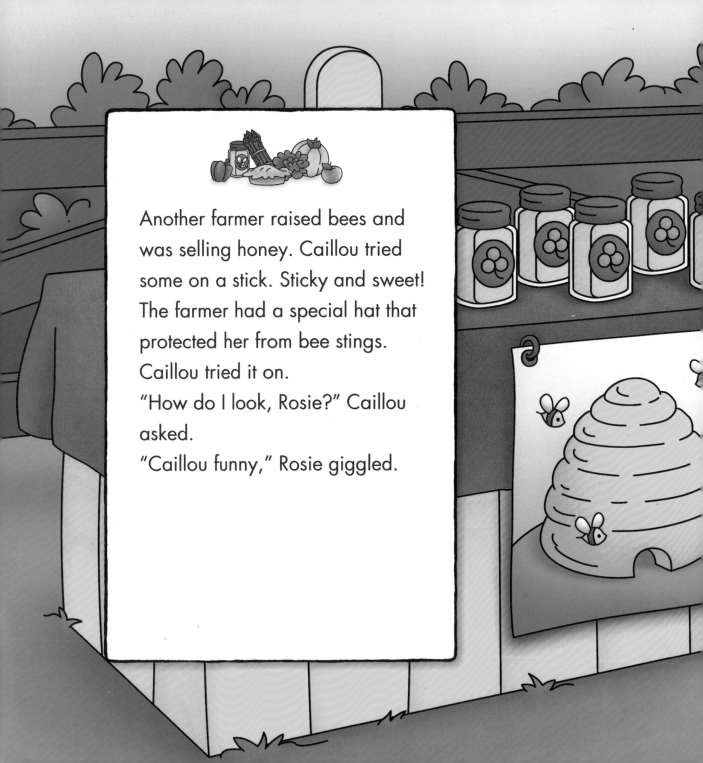

Another farmer raised bees and was selling honey. Caillou tried some on a stick. Sticky and sweet! The farmer had a special hat that protected her from bee stings. Caillou tried it on.

"How do I look, Rosie?" Caillou asked.

"Caillou funny," Rosie giggled.

At another table, Caillou saw
some long skinny vegetables.
"Mommy, what are those?"
he asked.
"Asparagus."
"As-par-a-gus! What a funny
name!" Caillou said it over and
over.
"Aspergoose!" Rosie laughed.
"Let's buy some," Mommy said.
"I have a wonderful recipe for
asparagus soup."

At home Mommy cut up the asparagus, cooked them in some water and then put everything in the blender.

"Would you like to push the button, Caillou?" she asked.

"Yes, please!" he said.

The mixture was green. Very green. Caillou wondered what it would taste like. What if he didn't like it?

At supper time, everyone loved the green soup. Even Rosie liked it.

Caillou wanted to visit the farmers' market again soon.

"We'll try another recipe when something else is in season," Daddy said.

"Can we cook something red next time?" Caillou said.

Text: Kim Thompson
Illustrations: Eric Sévigny
Art Direction: Monique Dupras

We acknowledge the financial support of the Government of Canada through
the Canada Book Fund for our publishing activities.

■✦■ Canadian   Patrimoine
      Heritage   canadien

We acknowledge the support of the Ministry of Culture and Communications
of Quebec and SODEC for the publication and promotion of this book.

SODEC ■■
Québec ■■

Bibliothèque et Archives nationales du Québec and Library
and Archives Canada cataloguing in publication

Thompson, Kim, 1964-
Caillou: fresh from the farm
(Ecology club)
For children aged 3 and up.

ISBN 978-2-89718-026-3

1. Farmers' markets - Juvenile literature. 2. Local foods - Juvenile literature.
3. Farm produce - Marketing - Juvenile literature. I. Sévigny, Éric. II. Title.
III. Title: Fresh from the farm. IV. Series: Ecology club.

HD9000.5.T46 2013   j381'.41   C2012-941688-6

The use of entirely recycled paper
produced locally, containing
chlorine-free 100% post-consumer
content, saved 22 mature trees.

Printed in Canada
10 9 8 7 6 5 4 3 2 1 CHO1866 JAN2013